For James Anatole
("with love and squalor")
—N.W.

For Julia Alvarez
—B.M.

East of the Sun

& West of the Moon

A PLAY BY
NANCY WILLARD

ILLUSTRATED BY BARRY MOSER

Harcourt Brace Jovanovich, Publishers
San Diego · New York · London

Library of Congress Cataloging-in-Publication Data
Willard, Nancy.
East of the sun and west of the moon: a play / by Nancy Willard;
illustrated by Barry Moser.—1st ed.
p. cm.
Summary: A girl travels east of the sun and west of the moon
to free her beloved prince from a magic spell.
ISBN 0-15-224750-5
1. Children's plays, American. [1. Fairy tales.   2. Folklore—
Norway.   3. Plays.]   I. Moser, Barry, Ill.   II. Title.
PS3573.I444E2 1989
812′.54—dc19   88-10903

First edition

A B C D E

The pictures in this book were painted with transparent watercolors
on paper handmade for the Royal Watercolour Society in 1982 by J. Barcham Greene.
The calligraphy is the work of Reassurance Wunder.
The text type was set in Sabon by Thompson Type, San Diego, California.
Color separations were made by Heinz Weber, Inc., Los Angeles, California.
Printed and bound by Tien Wah Press, Singapore
Production supervision by Warren Wallerstein and Rebecca Miller
Designed by Barry Moser, with thanks to Camilla Filancia

EAST OF THE SUN
&
WEST OF THE MOON

LIST OF CHARACTERS

PLAYERS

SOUTH WIND · EAST WIND · WEST WIND · NORTH WIND
WOODCUTTER · WOODCUTTER'S WIFE · ELDEST DAUGHTER
MIDDLE DAUGHTER · KAREN, *the Youngest Daughter* · BEAR / PRINCE
LONGNOSE, *the Troll Princess* · TROLL QUEEN · RAVEN · TROLL KING
CAPTIVE 1 · CAPTIVE 2 · CAPTIVE 3 · TROLLS

VOICES

CHAIR · TABLE · SPOON
KNIFE · COMB · RUG · DRESSES · BELL · HAM · HARP
WATER FOLK · BEASTS · BIRDS · STARS · ECHO

PUPPETS

KAREN · BEAR · all the WINDS
GOLDEN APPLE and SHEARS *that appear to move by themselves*

Note: Though the characters are many, they do not all appear on stage at once. One actor can play several different parts. The voices can be played by one or two people.

Scene: The set is simple, and the scenery is minimal. Changes of scene are indicated by "Lights up" on different parts of the set.

Act I *Scene I*

The set is marked like a compass with the North Wind, East Wind, South Wind, and West Wind. The Winds sit in their appropriate places. Lights up on the South Wind.

SOUTH WIND East Wind, West Wind! Where are you, sisters?

(Lights up on the East Wind)

EAST WIND I'm here, South Wind!

(Lights up on the West Wind)

WEST WIND And so am I!

SOUTH WIND Have you seen our brother, the North Wind?

(Lights up on the North Wind)

NORTH WIND Here I am, sisters.

SOUTH WIND Then let the story begin!

EAST WIND *(sings)*
>East of the sun and west of the moon,
>the Trolls will grind your bones into bread,
>or slobber you up with a silver spoon.
>Oh, the breath of a Troll can knock you dead,
>where the ice birds cry and the ice wolves run,
>west of the moon and east of the sun.

WEST WIND East of fire and north of water,
>the Woodcutter lives with his Wife and Daughters.
>The Oldest Daughter can weave and spin,
>but the Youngest can whistle and dance and sing.

NORTH WIND Karen can whistle and dance and sing.

SOUTH WIND The Middle Daughter can read and write.

EAST WIND But the Youngest makes up stories at night.

ALL THE WINDS Karen makes up stories at night.

SOUTH WIND North of their garden, south of their well,
>a bear is padding over the hill.
>East of the night and west of the storm,
>the poor Woodcutter is hurrying home.
>He's thinking of soup—there's none in the pot.
>He's thinking of bread—there's none in the box.

NORTH WIND   East of the lightning, west of the storm,
        The Troll Queen yells at her ugly daughter.

        (Yelling from offstage)

WEST WIND   The forest is full of such terrible things.
        The trees have tongues, and the rocks have wings.
        Shall we stir up the storm, shall we bellow a song
        to send the Woodcutter scurrying home?

EAST WIND   All roads lead home if you travel far enough.

NORTH WIND   Blow, blow, blow!

Scene II

    *Lights up on the living room of the Woodcutter's house. The door
    opens, and the Woodcutter hurries inside.*

WOODCUTTER   What a night! What a storm!
        I never saw worse since I was born.

        (He takes off his coat. His Wife hangs it up to dry.)

WIFE   Did you bring home some wood?

ELDEST DAUGHTER   Something we can sell for a lot of money? Did you,
        Papa?

KAREN   You're always worried about money. He's been out in this marvel-
        ous storm, and you worry about what he brought home. Papa, what
        was it like out in the storm?

WOODCUTTER   My axe broke. I couldn't bring home a single tree. And
        then the storm came.

        *(He pulls off his boots. His Wife takes them and pours the water out
        of them.)*

MIDDLE DAUGHTER   We're down to our last slice of bread, Papa.

WOODCUTTER   Again?

MIDDLE DAUGHTER   But the birds are eating well. Karen gave them half
        the loaf.

KAREN   You're always talking about food. Breakfast, lunch, dinner—that's
        all you ever think about.

WOODCUTTER   Did you give the birds half our loaf, Karen?

> (*The Wife takes the dishes out of the cupboard and begins to set the table for dinner.*)

KAREN   I had to give it to them, Papa. It's the only way to tame them.

ELDEST DAUGHTER   She stands outside for an hour holding a piece of bread in her hand while somebody else cooks the dinner.

KAREN   When the sparrows are tame, they sing so beautifully in the morning. I've often heard you say how much you enjoy their singing, Papa.

WOODCUTTER   It's true. I do love listening to the sparrows.

MIDDLE DAUGHTER   She goes outside and waits for the birds while somebody else washes the dishes.

KAREN   I hate washing dishes. The birds don't wash dishes. Why can't we live like the birds?

WIFE   All day long, that's what I have to put up with!

KAREN   Why can't we?

WOODCUTTER   Karen, I know you love the birds—

KAREN   I've finally got the chickadees eating from my hand—

WOODCUTTER   But there isn't enough food for everyone. There's just enough for us.

KAREN   The chickadees only eat crumbs. Little teeny crumbs.

WOODCUTTER   No more feeding the birds. Promise me, Karen.

KAREN   But what will I tell them?

WIFE   Tell them we're hungry. They'll understand.

WOODCUTTER   I'm famished. Let's eat. What do we have here? A slice of bread soaked in milk?

WIFE   We're out of milk again.

WOODCUTTER   Again?

ELDEST DAUGHTER   Karen has been feeding the cats.

WOODCUTTER   What cats? We don't have any cats.

ELDEST DAUGHTER   Lynxes, bobcats, tomcats—

MIDDLE DAUGHTER   Stray cats, tabby cats, fat cats. And not just cats (*lowering her voice*)—she's been feeding the bears.

WOODCUTTER   Bears! You're feeding the bears, Karen?

Karen

KAREN   Papa, they're such fun to watch.

ELDEST DAUGHTER   When Mama sends us out to pick blueberries, Karen leaves a little dish for the bears.

WOODCUTTER   Karen, do you realize how dangerous that is?

WIFE   I've told her, I've told her. It's like talking to a wall.

WOODCUTTER   A bear could tear me to pieces in minutes. They're the strongest animals in the forest.

MIDDLE DAUGHTER   And they're mean.

KAREN   Not the one I feed. He wouldn't hurt a fly.

WOODCUTTER   Promise you will stop feeding the bears.

KAREN   I—I—

WIFE   You *must* promise, Karen.

KAREN   I—I'll try not to do it anymore.

WOODCUTTER   Well, that's settled. Let's eat.

ELDEST DAUGHTER   One slice of bread for the five of us.

WOODCUTTER   You girls can have my share. I'm not hungry.

KAREN   But Papa, you're always hungry when you come home from the forest. And I'm not as hungry as I thought I was. We can divide my share.

WOODCUTTER   No, Karen, I can't take yours.

WIFE   We'll cut the slice into four parts.

(*She cuts the slice. The Woodcutter and his Daughters watch with great interest.*)

MIDDLE DAUGHTER   Yours is bigger.

ELDEST DAUGHTER   No, they're the same.

KAREN   Papa, where do the animals go in the storm?

WOODCUTTER   I didn't notice. The wind was tearing down trees.

WIFE   (*To the Eldest and the Middle Daughters*) We'll put it on four plates.

MIDDLE DAUGHTER   How come you get the plate with the flowers on it?

ELDEST DAUGHTER   You had it last time!

KAREN   (*dreamily*) The wind tearing down trees, what a sight that must be!

WOODCUTTER Sit down, my dears. Sit down and be still for a moment.
God who watches over us
bless this food to our use.

MIDDLE DAUGHTER And bring us more of it.

ELDEST DAUGHTER And better. And fresher.

KAREN And keep all travelers safe tonight.

WIFE Amen.

(Knock, knock, knock)

Who can that be?

MIDDLE DAUGHTER Hide the bread. We haven't enough for ourselves.

(Knock, knock, knock)

WOODCUTTER I'll answer it.

*(He opens the door. In steps a white Bear. The Middle and Eldest
Daughters scream and hide behind their mother. Karen stands beside
her father.)*

BEAR Good evening, Woodcutter.

WOODCUTTER Good evening to you. *(his voice trembles)* I—I suppose
you've come to escape the storm.

BEAR I have not come to escape the storm.

WOODCUTTER Ah! Perhaps—perhaps for a bit of supper, then?

BEAR I have not come for a bit of supper.

ELDEST DAUGHTER That's a mercy. Because we don't have any.

WIFE Not even for ourselves.

MIDDLE DAUGHTER We're poor, poor, poor!

BEAR I've come to make you rich, rich, rich.

MIDDLE DAUGHTER Rich?

BEAR As rich as you are now poor. Three meals a day. All the porkchops
and hamburgers you can eat.

WOODCUTTER Three meals a day?

BEAR All the clothes and toys you'll ever need. Coats, gowns, sneakers,
patent leathers, dolls, your own phone, your own TV . . .

ELDEST DAUGHTER A Bear giving me my own TV! You've got to be
kidding.

BEAR   With my deluxe magic purse, you'll have all the money you want.

MIDDLE DAUGHTER   That's crazy talk. Bears don't make people rich.

WIFE   Show us the purse.

(The Bear brings forth a jeweled purse.)

It's beautiful.

BEAR   Isn't it, though? And it's guaranteed to work forever. There's only one gift I want in return.

ELDEST DAUGHTER   What do you want?

MIDDLE DAUGHTER   Tell us.

BEAR   I want the Youngest girl in the room,
who sings with the sparrows and skips with the broom.
She doesn't wash dishes; she never scrubs floors;
she leans out the window and opens the doors.
Bread for the birds and milk for the cats—
all of us know her, the bears and the bats,
the fish and the fox, the deer and the otter.
She talks to the fire, she sings to the water.
I want the Woodcutter's Youngest Daughter.

WOODCUTTER   No!

ELDEST and MIDDLE DAUGHTERS   Yes!

(They rush over to Karen.)

BOTH DAUGHTERS   Three meals a day! Three meals a day!

MIDDLE DAUGHTER   Porkchops, pickles, popsicles, peppermint patties—

ELDEST DAUGHTER   Jackets, jeans, jacks, jump ropes—

BEAR   A new stove! Chairs with rungs! Everything brand new!

WIFE   Everything brand new?

MIDDLE DAUGHTER   Chicken wings, chitlins, chili dogs—

KAREN   No!

WOODCUTTER   So this is what comes of feeding bears!

ELDEST DAUGHTER   How can you be so selfish?

MIDDLE DAUGHTER   If you don't say yes, we'll starve to death.

BEAR   She won't come with me?

The Bear

WIFE   Let me talk to her, my Lord Bear. *(Aside to Karen)* Karen, think what this would mean to us. Your poor father's old and sick—is it right to make him go out in the storm and chop wood? Go with our visitor. He loves you.

KAREN   But, Mama, he's a Bear.

WIFE   But such a handsome Bear. And he has very nice manners.

WOODCUTTER   I will not allow Karen to go off with a Bear.

(He puts his arms around her protectively.)

WIFE   Talk to him, Karen. Give him a chance.

(Karen pulls away from her father. He watches, very upset.)

KAREN   Good evening, Lord Bear. What is it like out in the storm?

BEAR   The thunder roars, and the small birds cry.
But the roads I walk are quiet and dry.
I'll carry you east, I'll carry you west—
to the home of the Bear who loves you best.

WOODCUTTER   He'll kill you.

KAREN   Where is your home, Lord Bear?

BEAR   East of the forest, west of the storm,
nothing I carry shall come to harm.
The four Winds whistle and sing and clap,
and the seagulls sleep in the West Wind's lap.

KAREN   The seagulls asleep in the West Wind's lap—what a sight that must be. But I've never left home before.

BEAR   All roads lead home if you travel far enough.

KAREN   *(musing)* The four Winds clapping—what a sound that must be!

BEAR   Karen, will you come with me?

(A pause. Karen considers her answer.)

KAREN   I will.

BEAR   Climb on my back then.

(The Woodcutter runs forward and gives Karen a long hug.)

KAREN   Good-bye, Papa.

(Her mother and sisters also come forward and kiss her.)

KAREN   Good-bye, good-bye. Good-bye, water I carried; good-bye, fire I kept alive; good-bye, stars I wished on; good-bye, table and chair and little house in the woods. Good-bye, good-bye!

Scene III

Lights up on the great hall of the Trolls' castle. The Winds perch on the four corners of the set, left and right, high and low.

EAST WIND East of the sun and west of the moon,
the Trolls are brewing a terrible storm.

SOUTH WIND They've dishes of diamonds, silver, and gold,
but the diamonds are tough, and the silver is cold.

WEST WIND The Troll Queen's daughter is lazy and fat.

LONGNOSE Bring me this, Mother, bring me that!

TROLL QUEEN We have too many uncles and cousins and cats.
They drop in for breakfast, they drop in for dinner.
They're growing fatter, and I'm growing thinner.

LONGNOSE Wash my clothes, Mother. Mend the holes!

TROLL QUEEN I hate cleaning up after slobbery Trolls.
And I'm stuck with a daughter
who hates soap and water.
Your hair is all greasy, your dress is in rags,
You look like the devil's old racketty hags.
What will your Prince say?

LONGNOSE What does it matter? He's not mine yet.

Scene IV

Lights down on the Trolls, lights up on the Winds and a scene in the distance, done with puppets, of Karen and the Bear on the road.

EAST WIND Listen, listen!

SOUTH WIND Look, look!

WEST WIND East of the storm and west of the rain,
the white Bear's hurrying home again.

EAST WIND Who's that on his back?

SOUTH WIND The Woodcutter's Daughter.

WEST WIND How beautiful she is!

NORTH WIND How small she is!

SOUTH WIND How noisy she is!

(Sound of Karen and the Bear laughing together)

Puppet scene fades. Lights up on Karen and the Bear on the road in the woods. They walk in place. Scenery is pulled past them to suggest motion.

KAREN *(sings)* When you go through the forest at midnight,
and your friends and relations are few,
just remember the crow and the cricket
are twice as nervous as you.
Just remember the Bear who brings you
knows all the best people by name;
the sun and the moon are friendly,
and so is the wind and the rain.

BEAR The sun and the moon are friendly,
and so is the wind and the rain.

KAREN Are we almost there?

BEAR Not yet. *(sings)*
Let the North Wind bellow and bluster.
He's nice when you meet him inside.
The lightning wears rings on her fingers.
The Winds take the sparrows for rides;
they love to jump puddles and gather
umbrellas and hats in the rain.
Blow from the east, and blow from the west!
Blow till we're home again!

KAREN How far is it now?

BEAR Far and not far. Do you see anything?

KAREN I see a mountain.

BEAR We're going through that mountain.

(They pass through the mountain.)

KAREN Are we there yet?

BEAR Not yet.

KAREN How far is it?

BEAR It's not far now. Do you see anything?

KAREN Only the sky.

BEAR Do you see anything *now?*

KAREN I see something sparkling and twinkling. It looks like a tiny, tiny star.

The Bear's Palace

BEAR It's not so tiny.

KAREN It's shining like the moon.

BEAR That's no moon.

KAREN It's shining like the sun.

BEAR That's my palace.

KAREN A palace. You didn't tell me you live in a palace.

BEAR You didn't ask me.

KAREN It doesn't look like a palace when you get up close.

BEAR What do you see?

KAREN I see a pile of stones.

BEAR Climb down from my back, Karen. Pick up one black stone and one white stone. Now strike them together.

Scene VI

She does so, and her room in the palace appears. The pile of stones are now part of a golden fountain in a courtyard, furnished with a Table, Chair, dishes, vanity table, and mirror.

FURNITURE Welcome, Karen, to your new home!

CHAIR I am the Chair, your golden Chair. When you are tired, sit on me.

TABLE I am your golden Table. When you eat your supper, eat on me.

SPOON I am your golden Spoon. I shall always serve you.

KNIFE I am your golden Knife, a cut above the Spoon.

COMB I am your golden Comb. I love your hair.

RUG I am your Carpet. I worship the ground you walk on.

DRESSES We are your Dresses, and we are all beautiful.

KAREN How beautiful you are! Thank you, all of you.

BELL I am your Bell. I can call all the others.

BEAR Whenever you wish for anything, Karen, ring the Bell, and it will appear. You can have anything you wish. Look around and enjoy yourself. I've got to be moving on.

KAREN Aren't you going to stay?

BEAR Bears don't live in palaces.

KAREN Why do you have one then?

BEAR For you. Girls don't live in forests.

KAREN I love the forest. I'd love to live in the forest.

(The Bell rings. Through the walls of the palace shines a forest. Suddenly a peal of thunder shakes everything.)

KAREN But when it rains, I'd rather live in a palace.

(The forest fades.)

This place takes my breath away. Will I stay here all by myself?

BEAR Every evening I'll visit you, to see if you are happy. Do you think you can be happy?

KAREN Oh, yes.

BEAR Good-bye, Karen.

(Exit the Bear.)

KAREN Let's see if the Bell really works. I'm hungry.

(She rings the Bell. The supper assembles itself. The Chair draws itself out for her.)

HAM Here I am! Am I cooked well enough for you?

KAREN You look delicious. May I—may I—?

HAM Eat your supper? Nothing would please me more.

KAREN It's so quiet here. I wish I had some music.

(Music. She eats her supper.)

How sleepy I am! I wonder where the bedroom is? I'm so tired—I wish the bed were right here this minute.

(The bed appears.)

What a bed! Clean sheets, soft pillows. I hope the mattress is nice and bouncy.

(She bounces up and down on the mattress.)

Oh, I forgot to pack my nightgown. Oh!

(She finds herself in a splendid nightgown.)

Why, this is so lovely I could go dancing in it.

(She crawls into bed.)

I wish I had an extra blanket.

(The blanket arrives.)

And someone to sing me to sleep.

(The Harp arrives.)

HARP *(sings)* Lullaby, little Karen.
You have traveled far.
East of the farthest cottage,
west of the nearest star.
South of the full moon rising,
north of the morning light.
Lullaby, little traveler.
Go to sleep, good night.

KAREN That's wonderful. Whoever you are, wherever you are *(the Furniture laughs)*, I wonder if you could bring me my teddy bear? *(Laughter again)* Well, I suppose even a magic Bell can't grant all wishes. But I do miss my bear. And I'll bet he misses me. Who will he sleep with tonight?

(She falls asleep. In pads the white Bear and slips off his skin. Transformed into the Prince, he climbs into bed.)

Act II   *Scene I*

Lights up on the Winds, lights down on the palace.

ALL THE WINDS East of summer and west of fall,
Karen lives in the great white hall.

BELL What do you wish for? What do you choose?

KAREN'S VOICE Roller skates and running shoes.

NORTH WIND And every night while Karen sleeps,
into her bed the white Bear creeps.

SOUTH WIND He leaves his bearskin on the floor.

EAST WIND And in the morning, he's out the door.

WEST WIND What do you wish for? What do you choose?

The Brewing Storm

(Lights up on Karen. To suggest passing of time, Karen skips rope while behind her, the moon comes out. Gradually the palace grows lighter and lighter, till the sun comes up. Then the palace grows dark once more. This happens in rapid succession five times. Karen continues to skip.)

Scene II

Lights up on Karen's room. The Bell rings, Karen sits at her Table, and the dinner appears.

BEAR *(To Karen at dinner)* Are you happy, Karen?

ECHO Are you happy, Karen? Happy Karen happy Karen happy Karen. . . .

KAREN *(sings)* I have hundreds of dresses; the food is fine;
I live in a palace where everything's mine.
But I often dream of my home in the woods,
and bread soaked in milk—oh, it tasted so good!
And my sisters gabbing, and the fire so bright
when I told my sisters stories at night,
and my mother dividing the last of the bread,
and the thankful blessing my father said.

BEAR Then you aren't happy, Karen? You don't have everything you want?

KAREN I'm sort of happy. But if I could go home, just for a visit, I'd be *really* happy.

BEAR It's a long trip.

KAREN I know.

BEAR And there's a storm brewing.

KAREN I've been in storms before.

BEAR And it's cold.

KAREN I've been cold before. Oh, please let me go home. I'm so lonely.

BEAR It's true you never see another soul during the day except me.

KAREN If I could just go home for a day.

BEAR Will that make you happy?

KAREN Oh, yes, yes!

BEAR I'll miss you terribly.

KAREN I'll only stay a week.

BEAR A whole week! I'll be miserable.

KAREN Oh, please, please.

BEAR I might even get sick.

KAREN Please. I want to go home. I have to go home.

BEAR If I carry you home, I want you to promise me something.

KAREN What?

BEAR Don't let your mother get you alone.

KAREN I promise.

BEAR Talk to her only when the others are near.

KAREN I promise.

BEAR Even when she takes your hand and leads you upstairs to show you the new guestroom.

KAREN I promise.

BEAR Very well. I'll carry you home for a visit.

KAREN Wheeee!

BEAR But remember, if you break your promise, you'll bring bad luck on us both.

KAREN I promise, I promise.

Scene III

Lights up on road in the forest. Karen and the Bear are traveling in place, while the scenery is pulled past them.

ALL THE WINDS East of sorrow and west of joy,
    the white Bear follows a starlit track
    with the Woodcutter's Daughter—he's taking her back.

SOUTH WIND How beautiful she is!

WEST WIND How small she is!

EAST WIND How happy she is!

KAREN *(sings)* When you're going back home through the forest,
    and the road feels lonely and long,
    the violets will lay you a carpet,
    and the sparrows will pipe you a song,
    and a Bear is just one of the family
    if you know your relations by name.

Blow from the east, and blow from the west,
and blow till we're home again!

(Snow falls.)

BEAR   How different the world looks covered with snow. I've never made this trip in winter. I've never seen so much snow.

KAREN   I have. My sisters and I used to make snow angels.

BEAR   Snow angels?

KAREN   You lie down in the snow and flap your arms—

BEAR   The road is gone. Maybe we've lost our way.

KAREN   No, we haven't. All roads lead to home if you travel far enough. I could find this road in my sleep.

BEAR   Everything is asleep except us. Are we nearly there?

KAREN   Not yet.

BEAR   How far is it?

KAREN   Far and not far.

(Snow stops falling.)

Look—there ahead of us! What do you see?

BEAR   I see a large house with a barn.

KAREN   So do I. But we didn't have a barn. What else do you see?

BEAR   I see a field with cows grazing.

KAREN   So do I. But we didn't have a field, and we didn't have cows. What else do you see?

BEAR   Chimneys puffing, bread cooling on the sill, dresses flapping on the clothesline.

KAREN   So many lovely dresses. We never had that many dresses.

BEAR   And in front of the house, an old man is weeping in his silver chair, his axe propped up beside him. And nothing his Wife offers him makes him happy.

KAREN   That's my father and mother!

BEAR   I'll come back for you in a week. Remember your promise.

KAREN   I'll remember. Papa! Papa! Mama!

(The Bear lumbers away.)

WOODCUTTER   Karen!

(He runs to Karen and hugs her.)

WIFE   I can't believe my eyes!

BEAR'S VOICE   *(Offstage)* Don't forget your promise!

The Woodcutter

Scene IV

The Woodcutter, Wife, Eldest Daughter, and Middle Daughter rush out. They gather around Karen.

WOODCUTTER, WIFE, ELDEST and MIDDLE DAUGHTERS Where did you come from? Where do you live? Palace or cottage? Castle or cave?

MIDDLE DAUGHTER What do you cook—and what do you eat?

KAREN Popcorn and celery, cornflakes and beets, ice cream and carrots, cocoa and tea.

WOODCUTTER How did you travel? By land or by sea?

ELDEST DAUGHTER Who cleans the kitchen? Who are your friends?

WIFE Who says goodnight when the daylight ends?

KAREN I have a nice house, I have my own room,
I don't wash dishes, I don't touch the broom.
The white Bear is faithful, loving, and kind.
Whatever I wish for, I ask, and it's mine.

WIFE Karen, can I talk with you alone?

KAREN Later, later.

ELDEST DAUGHTER Karen, come upstairs.

(*Lights up inside of the Woodcutter's cottage, which is now beautifully furnished.*)

This is my room. Everything matches.

MIDDLE DAUGHTER This is my TV. Every room in the house has one.

ELDEST DAUGHTER This is my new bike. It has thirty-two speeds and a radio and it glows in the dark.

MIDDLE DAUGHTER Look out the window. That's my new pony.

KAREN Amazing. Simply amazing.

WIFE Karen, come and see how we've fixed up the guestroom.

KAREN Later, later.

(*The Eldest Daughter and Middle Daughter exit.*)

WIFE Karen, what is it? You can tell me.

KAREN I'm not hiding anything.

WIFE   You haven't said a word about who lives in the palace with you. Surely you don't live there alone?

KAREN   I'm alone during the day.

WIFE   And at night?

KAREN   I can't tell you. I promised.

WIFE   Who did you promise?

KAREN   The white Bear.

WIFE   The white Bear comes to you at night?

KAREN   Not a Bear. A man.

WIFE   What man?

KAREN   I don't know.

WIFE   You don't know! What's his name?

KAREN   I don't know his name. I think he's a Prince.

WIFE   You *think* he's a Prince—and you don't know his name? What does he look like?

KAREN   I don't know.

WIFE   You don't know what he looks like?

KAREN   He told me never to look at him. If I do, something dreadful will happen. It's always dark when he comes.

WIFE   Why, he may be a Troll!

KAREN   *(indignantly)*   He's not a Troll.

WIFE   He may be planning to eat you alive.

KAREN   Oh, no, he loves me.

WIFE   You can never trust a Troll.

KAREN   He's not a Troll. *(in a doubtful voice)* I don't think he's a Troll.

WIFE   There's only one way to be sure. I'll give you a bit of candle. Light it when he's asleep.

KAREN   But he said I should never, never try to find out what he looks like.

WIFE   Then he *must* be a Troll. Do you want to spend the rest of your life with a Troll?

KAREN   But he said—

WIFE   If you look at him when he's asleep, he'll never suspect a thing. Just be careful not to drop any hot wax on him.

KAREN   But—

WIFE   He'll never know, I tell you. Be very careful about the wax.

Scene V

Lights up on puppets of the Bear and Karen. Music.

ALL THE WINDS   East of the stars and west of the moon, the Bear is carrying Karen home.

Scene VI

Lights up on Karen's room in the Bear's palace. Karen mimes the story as it is told by the East Wind.

EAST WIND   West of the living and north of the dead,
Karen crawls into her golden bed.
The sheets are silk, and the bed is wide.
And the man whose face she has never seen
takes his place at his sweetheart's side.
And when she's certain he's fast asleep
(not even the moon has seen her creep),
and only the sight of his face can save her,
she lights the candle her mother gave her.

KAREN   How beautiful he is!

FURNITURE   How beautiful he is!

KAREN   You are the handsomest Prince in the world.

FURNITURE   The handsomest Prince in the world.

KAREN   If I don't give you one small kiss, I can't live another minute.

FURNITURE   Another minute, another minute.

(Three drops of wax fall. As each drop strikes the Prince's skin, a gong sounds, and each time he gives a sudden jerk, as if the wax burns him.)

PRINCE   *(Springing up)*   What have you done? What have you done?

KAREN   I—I wanted to see you.

PRINCE   Ah, Karen, you've ruined us both.

KAREN   Ruined us?

PRINCE   If only you'd held out for one more day, I'd be free.

KAREN   Free of what? What are you talking about?

PRINCE   Free from the Troll Queen's spell. She wants me to marry her daughter.

The Prince

KAREN   A spell!

PRINCE   *(chanting the spell for her)*
> A bear by day, a man by night.
> If you step from dark to light
> before another year unrolls,
> you shall live among the Trolls.

VOICE OF THE TROLL QUEEN   *(Offstage)*
> You shall wed my only daughter.
> Earth, air, fire, water!
> To your wedding you must fly.

PRINCE AND VOICE OF THE TROLL QUEEN
> Linger here and you shall die.

KAREN   Oh, why didn't you tell me? Why didn't you tell me?

PRINCE   I couldn't. That was part of the spell. And now I'm off to the Troll people, for the Troll Princess is waiting for me. She has a nose three feet long, and she's the wife I must have now.

KAREN   Can't I go with you?

PRINCE   No, you can't.

KAREN   Tell me the way, and I'll look for you.

PRINCE   Oh, my dear, there's no way for you to get to that place. It lies east of the sun and west of the moon, and you'll never find it. The Troll Queen is calling me—I can feel it in my legs—I can't stay—good bye, Karen, good-bye.

Scene VII

The Prince vanishes. Lights up on puppet of Karen in the woods.

ALL THE WINDS   *(sing)*
> East of sorrow and west of grief,
> Karen woke on the chilly ground.
> Magic is a cunning thief.
> The palace sank without a sound.
> Golden fountain, golden Chair,
> golden Comb that loved her hair,
> golden bed in golden room,
> golden Knife and golden Spoon,

friendly Bell—they've up and gone
east of wish and west of none.
Look, look, look!
The Woodcutter's Daughter is walking, walking.
What's that in her hand?
A little stick.
How small she is!
How quiet she is!
How tired she is.

(*Puppet of Karen walks uphill and down.*)

VOICE OF KAREN (*sings*)
The road across the mountains
is neither smooth nor wide.
But I hear someone whistling
on the other side.

Scene VIII

Lights up on the South Wind's house as Karen arrives. The South Wind lives in a small cottage at the edge of a stream. Beside the cottage is an apple tree loaded with golden apples. The South Wind is a housekeeping enthusiast. She sweeps the stairs. She sweeps the rocking chair on her porch. She sweeps her front walk. She sweeps the grass right down to the water, and she sweeps the water. A Golden Apple follows her like a mischievous kitten.

SOUTH WIND (*To the Apple*) Out of my way, out of my way! You're always underfoot. And all those blossoms and leaves you bring in—why can't you clean up after yourself?

KAREN Good evening. Can you tell me where I am?

SOUTH WIND I am the South Wind, and this is my very clean house. Can you scrub floors?

KAREN I—

SOUTH WIND Wash dishes?

KAREN Well—

SOUTH WIND Can you sweep?

KAREN Yes!

SOUTH WIND   Good. You can sweep my front porch. Now let me tell you about this broom. If you stay on its good side, it'll do anything for you. If you hurt its feelings, you won't get a lick of work out of it.

(She hands Karen the broom. Karen sweeps.)

Careful you don't hurt its feelings. That broom can be really nasty to strangers.

KAREN   Brooms don't have feelings.

(The broom shrinks; Karen continues sweeping till she is practically on her knees.)

SOUTH WIND   That's no way to sweep. Why, it'll take you a year to clean my porch at the rate you're going.

KAREN   If I just had a bigger broom—

(The broom grows; Karen continues sweeping but with difficulty.)

SOUTH WIND   I don't know why you want to make a mountain out of a molehole.

KAREN   I don't know why this broom doesn't behave itself.

SOUTH WIND   You insulted it. You should apologize.

KAREN   Apologize? To a broom?

SOUTH WIND   Of course. You can say, "I'm sorry, broom."

KAREN   I'm sorry, broom.

(The broom leaps from Karen's hands and sweeps like mad.)

SOUTH WIND   What did I tell you?

KAREN   What a wonderful broom! I wish my mother had a broom like this.

(The broom drops.)

Oh, what's wrong with it?

SOUTH WIND   It got tired, of course. Same as you would.

(She leans the broom against the house.)

KAREN   I'm tired, too. I've been walking for such a long time. May I sit here and rest?

SOUTH WIND   Yes, if you don't muss anything. Don't make dust, don't leave tracks, don't break anything, don't touch anything. Put everything back where you found it, and don't track sunlight all over my nice clean yard.

(Karen sits in the rocking chair while the South Wind fetches a mop

South Wind

and bucket and starts mopping down the porch. Karen lifts first one foot and then the other to accommodate her.)

It's never and never I've had a young girl come by here. I suppose you've lost something?

KAREN Yes, I'm looking for—

SOUTH WIND Your hat, your umbrella, your clean sheets off the clothesline? I never take sheets off people's clotheslines. I take nothing but socks. One of each kind, that's what I take.

KAREN I'm looking for the Prince who's gone to marry the Troll Princess with a nose three feet long.

SOUTH WIND How did you know about him? Are you the girl that should have had him?

KAREN I am, oh, I am! Do you know where I can find him?

SOUTH WIND I haven't the faintest idea.

KAREN *(disappointed)* Oh.

SOUTH WIND Perhaps the Water Folk can help you.

KAREN What Water Folk?

SOUTH WIND The Folk that live in the lakes and the rivers and the sea. I am the mistress of all that lives in the waters. The whale and the porpoise, the salmon and the trout, the catfish and carp—oh, there isn't a family alive I don't know by name. Believe me, I'm the grandmother of thousands. And every evening Folk from each of the great oceans gather here and bring me news of the world.

KAREN Will they be here soon?

SOUTH WIND No. But if I whistle for them, they'll come directly.

(She blows the whistle that hangs around her neck. There is a rustling and chattering as the Water Folk arrive. The Water Folk are painted on a transparent screen; they appear when it is lit from behind.)

Children of the waters! Listen to me!

WATER FOLK We're listening, Grandmother.

SOUTH WIND One of the land people has come to me.

(Whispers of astonishment from the Water Folk)

She has a question for you.

KAREN I'm looking for the Prince that's gone to marry the Troll Princess with a nose three feet long. Do any of you know where I can find him?

(A great murmur rises among the Water Folk.)

SOUTH WIND Whale, have you seen him?

WHALE Not I, Grandmother.

SOUTH WIND Shark, what about you?

SHARK No, Grandmother.

SOUTH WIND You haven't eaten him, I hope.

SHARK No. But if I meet him—watch out!

SOUTH WIND Salmon? Porpoise? Sea Turtle? Trout?

(As she calls the names, they answer, "No.")

Lobster?

LOBSTER Not I. But one of my brothers escaped from a Troll-trap in the waters east of the sun and west of the moon, and now that I think of it, he did say something about a Prince who lives in the Trolls' castle.

KAREN The Trolls' castle—that's where I'm going. Do you know the way?

LOBSTER I wouldn't be caught dead there. But my brother said he passed the house of the East Wind on the way back. Perhaps she can help you.

SOUTH WIND The East Wind? I haven't visited my sister in years.

KAREN Where does the East Wind live?

SOUTH WIND Oh, it's a long journey to my sister's house, over sand and sea, towers and turtles, moonbeams and millstones—

KAREN A long journey—and I'm already so tired I can hardly move.

SOUTH WIND —over wishes and windmills. Take my Golden Apple. Hold it in your hand, and you won't feel tired at all.

KAREN Thank you. It's lovely, but I hate to—

SOUTH WIND Take it. The backyard is full of them. Mushing underfoot, cluttering up my nice clean grass.

KAREN It's beautiful. I wish I had a pocket. Where can I hide it so no one will steal it?

SOUTH WIND No one can take this Apple from you unless you give it away yourself.

(Karen takes the Apple.)

KAREN How strange. A minute ago I was too tired to stand, but now I feel as if I'd had a good night's sleep. Is this the road to your sister's house?

SOUTH WIND It is, but you'll be an old woman before you arrive if you follow that road. Hop on my cloak, and I'll take you there myself. Back to your waters, my children!

KAREN Thank you, all of you—good-bye!

WATER FOLK Good-bye, earth-sister! Good-bye! Good-bye!

Scene IX

Lights up on puppets of Karen and the South Wind traveling through the air.

SOUTH WIND *(sings)*
When you reach the mountain,
never turn away.
Who knows what awaits us
at the rim of day?
A giant with a toothache
gnawing a dragonbone?
A green-haired woman playing
a Golden Comb?

(Lights up on a gazebo in the East Wind's garden. Unlike most gazebos, this one contains a chest full of clothes. The lid is open; the East Wind has been trying them on. Dressed in a shimmering robe, she is sitting before an empty frame that once held a mirror. She is combing her green hair with a Golden Comb. At each stroke, flowers fall out of her hair.)

SOUTH WIND Sister!

EAST WIND Who's there? I'm not expecting visitors.

SOUTH WIND Has it been that long since we've seen each other? I hope you haven't forgotten your own sister.

EAST WIND Oh, Lord—I haven't had a visitor in years, and now when I get one, I'm hardly fit to be seen.

KAREN You look beautiful to me.

EAST WIND Who are you?

East Wind

SOUTH WIND   This is the lass who should have had the Prince who lives in the Trolls' castle.

KAREN   Please—won't you tell me how to find him? The Lobster thought you might know.

EAST WIND   What Lobster? What Prince? I'm all befuddled. Ever since I broke my mirror, I hardly know whether I'm coming or going.

SOUTH WIND   *(whispering to Karen)* She's helpless without her mirror. Can you be a mirror? Just for a few minutes?

KAREN   I've never tried it. What should I do?

SOUTH WIND   Just step behind that frame and do exactly as she does.

KAREN   But won't she know the difference?

SOUTH WIND   No, she's awfully nearsighted. She'll see what she wants to see. Hurry.

(Karen steps behind the empty frame. The East Wind catches sight of her.)

EAST WIND   Oh, there I am! I feel so much better knowing where I stand. Now, what shall I wear?

SOUTH WIND   *(Reaching for a dress from the chest)* How about this green dress?

(The East Wind tries it on, poses before the mirror. A green light falls on Karen, who imitates every gesture.)

EAST WIND   Too tight. I've put on five pounds. I need something large and billowy.

SOUTH WIND   Here's a big blue thing. Just the shade of my whales.

(The East Wind tries on the blue tent dress and turns a few waltz steps with an imaginary partner, humming. A blue light falls on Karen, who does exactly the same thing.)

EAST WIND   Do you think it brings out the real me?

SOUTH WIND   That's asking too much of any dress. Put it on. It looks fine.

EAST WIND   No, it doesn't. Blue never was my color. How about this yellow one?

SOUTH WIND   It's fine, it's fine. Hurry up, can't you?

EAST WIND   I haven't a thing to wear. Not a thing.

SOUTH WIND   Nonsense! You're always stealing dresses from people's clotheslines.

EAST WIND I don't steal them. I borrow them. When I'm tired of a dress, I take it back.

SOUTH WIND You don't.

EAST WIND I do.

SOUTH WIND You don't.

EAST WIND I do.

KAREN (*Stepping through the frame*) Oh, please don't fight.

SOUTH WIND Yes, let's not fight, sister. We're here on important business. We're looking for that Prince.

EAST WIND What Prince?

KAREN The one who's gone east of the sun and west of the moon.

EAST WIND Why, he rushed by here a long time ago. Are you the lass that should have had him?

KAREN I am. Can you tell me how to find him?

EAST WIND No. But perhaps the Beasts can help you.

KAREN Beasts?

EAST WIND I am mistress of all the Beasts that live on land. The deer, the bear, the tiger, the elephant—they come when I call them. Once a day the Beasts of the desert and the Beasts of the mountain and the Beasts of the forest and the Beasts of the plains send some of their children to bring me news of the world.

SOUTH WIND Call the Beasts, sister.

(*The East Wind takes a ram's horn from a hook in the gazebo and blows it. The Beasts are painted on a transparent screen; like the Water Folk, they appear when lit from behind.*)

EAST WIND Beloved Beasts, a human being has found her way to my house. She has a question for you.

KAREN I'm looking for the Prince that's gone east of the sun and west of the moon to marry the Troll Princess with a nose three feet long. Can you help me find the way?

EAST WIND Otter, have you seen him?

OTTER No, Grandmother.

EAST WIND Moose, how about you?

MOOSE I've seen many fine sights in my time, but never a Prince, Grandmother.

KAREN   Nobody? Nobody has seen him? Nobody knows the way to the castle?

(Silence. When the Flea speaks, he is so tiny that nobody sees him.)

FLEA   Listen to me! Listen to me!

MOOSE   Who's talking?

FLEA   I'm a Flea!

KAREN   I don't see anyone.

FLEA   I am a wise and charming Flea!

KAREN   Where are you?

FLEA   Right here, on the back of the Moose.

MOOSE   A Flea on my back? I thought I felt someone biting—

SOUTH WIND   Hush, let the Flea speak.

FLEA   My sister lived on one of the Trolls for a year and barely escaped with her life. You wouldn't want to meet them. They have huge teeth and claws.

KAREN   I know.

FLEA   The Queen roars. The Princess screams. And she has a nose three feet long. The Troll castle is a terrible place.

KAREN   I know. How do I get there?

FLEA   She never told me, and I never asked.

KAREN   Oh, can't any of you help me?

FLEA   It seems to me that my sister said something about the West Wind. Something about passing the house of the West Wind on her way back.

EAST WIND   I haven't visited her for years.

SOUTH WIND   Neither have I. Remember when we were young, all of us no bigger than a breeze? She was so daring. She'd fly to the end of the world and back before lunch.

EAST WIND   She always was a regular tomboy.

KAREN   Do you think she'll help me?

EAST WIND   She might. But you can't go visiting if you're all rumpled up. I'll give you my Comb. If you feel lonely, comb with the silver side.

(The East Wind combs Karen's hair.)

West Wind

KAREN   How strange! Suddenly I can remember way, way back to when I was a baby. I remember my first doll. My first sneakers. My first word.

SOUTH WIND   What was your first word?

KAREN   It was "why."

EAST WIND   Oh, you're ready now, I expect. But it's a fearful journey. You'll be frightened, I know. That's when you should comb with the gold side.

KAREN   *(Repeating the East Wind's instructions)* If I'm lonely, I comb with the silver side. If I'm frightened, I comb with the gold side. Thank you. I'll be very careful of the Comb.

EAST WIND   Don't worry. No one can take it from you unless you give it away yourself. Climb aboard my cape.

KAREN   It's a lovely cape. Very becoming to you.

EAST WIND   Do you like it? I think it makes a bold statement. It's real silk that's been dipped in magic.

FLEA   I hope you find your Prince.

MOOSE   Go well, little human.

BEASTS   Good-bye, good-bye!

KAREN   Good-bye—thank you, South Wind, for everything—good-bye!

Act III   *Scene 1*

Lights down on the East Wind's gazebo. Lights up on the West Wind's tent. The sky is black. The tent is transparent. It is pitched on a rocky desert. The wind is blowing; from time to time the wind rises, and the speakers must shout to be heard. The West Wind wears a pair of Golden Shears around her neck and is attended by a Raven. She is lighting the Stars over her tent with a long pole, which she dips into a campfire. Wherever her pole touches the sky, a Star lights up. Roar of wind is heard offstage. Enter the East Wind and Karen.

WEST WIND   Blow, blow, blow! What brings you to this wild place, sister?

EAST WIND   A girl in search of a Prince.

WEST WIND   *(To the Raven)* Can't hear a thing. What did she say?

RAVEN   A churl in search of a pinch.

WEST WIND   Honest? That's what she said?

RAVEN   A curl in search of a cinch.

WEST WIND   Tell me the truth or I'll clip your wings. *(She snaps the Shears.)*

RAVEN   Oh, don't clip my wings, Grandmother! I was only joking. I'll tell you the truth: we have visitors. And one of them is a girl in search of a Prince.

WEST WIND   I don't believe you.

RAVEN   Seeing is believing, Grandmother. There she is.

KAREN   I'm looking for a Prince. I thought you might know how to find him.

WEST WIND   A Prince? Only one Prince has passed this way, and he was going to his wedding.

KAREN   I'm the one he should be marrying! I'm the one that should have had him! Not that Princess with the nose three feet long, not that terrible Troll—

STARS   *Troll! (All the Stars shriek and go out.)*

WEST WIND   *(very much annoyed)* Now look what you've done. You scared away the light.

KAREN   I'm awfully sorry.

WEST WIND   It'll take all night to light those Stars again.

(*She starts lighting them, one at a time.*)

EAST WIND   *(whispering)* Have you no manners at all? You can't expect her to help you if you behave like such an oaf.

KAREN   *(whispering)* I'm sorry. How did I know the Stars would go out when I said the word Troll—

(*Two Stars shriek and go out. The West Wind lights them again.*)

RAVEN   Stars are so timid. Now if you'd said roll or mole or hole, they wouldn't have blinked an eye. But Troll—

(*Two other Stars shriek and go out. The rest sigh and flicker.*)

WEST WIND   I don't know what's got into these Stars.

EAST WIND   *(To Karen and the Raven)* I don't want to hear that word again from either of you.

(Having re-lit the Stars, the West Wind turns back to her guests.)

WEST WIND   What were we speaking of? A Prince?

KAREN   Yes, the one who's gone east of the sun and west of the moon to marry a Tro— a large monstrous person. Can you help me find him?

WEST WIND   I've never blown that far in my life. The Tr— large monstrous persons live farther than the end of the world. I don't think anyone has ever come back from that place alive.

RAVEN   If you want to find the road to the castle of the large monstrous persons, why don't you ask the Birds? They ride the currents of heaven; they see all roads.

WEST WIND   Of course—the Birds will know. I'll fetch my drum.

(She brings a drum out of the tent and thumps on it like a heartbeat. As with the Water Folk and the Beasts, the Birds arrive by means of a transparent screen lit from behind.)

BIRDS   Grandmother, Grandmother, what do you want? Why have you called us from the air over the desert, and the air over the forests, and the air over the water, and the air over the plains?

WEST WIND   One of your wingless sisters has come to me. She has a question for you.

KAREN   I'm looking for the Prince that's gone east of the sun and west of the moon to marry the Princess with a nose three feet long. Tell me if you can—where is the road to that place? *(Silence)*

WEST WIND   Owl, you are the wisest of my children. Can you help this girl?

OWL   I have heard it said the nights there are so dark you can lose yourself for hundreds of years. Also, the mice are all scrawny. Owls do not travel in that country.

WEST WIND   Sea gull, you make your bed on the chilly sea—can you help this girl?

SEA GULL   No. The waters around that country would kill us.

PENGUIN   Take my advice, wingless one—don't go.

PARROT   It's a terrible place. You'll have none of the comforts of home.

KAREN   I know that.

WEST WIND   Nightingale, did you want to say something?

The Winds' Gifts to Karen

NIGHTINGALE What does she care about the comforts of home? All roads lead home if your Prince is waiting at the end of them.

WEST WIND But who can show her the way?

CANADA GOOSE What about your brother, the North Wind?

ALL THE BIRDS *(exclaim)* The North Wind! Oh, he's a wild one! (etc.)

WEST WIND I haven't visited him for years. Have you, sister?

EAST WIND I wouldn't dream of visiting our brother. His idea of a good time is going out and sinking a couple of ships.

WEST WIND Or blowing away a dozen rooftops.

CANADA GOOSE But he could help the wingless one.

WEST WIND He could. But he's so bad-tempered.

EAST WIND He's the strongest of us.

WEST WIND And the meanest.

EAST WIND And the oldest.

KAREN I want to meet him.

WEST WIND If *he* doesn't know the way, you'll never find anyone in the world to tell you. But it's a long, cold journey to his place. You'll need a warm cloak. *(She takes the Golden Shears from her belt.)*
Snip the thread,
and whip the thread.
Crick crack croak!
Make this girl a cloak!
(The Shears snip and snap, and they make her a cloak.)
Do you like silver buttons?

KAREN Silver buttons are very nice.

SHEARS *(whispering)* Buttons buttons buttons buttons buttons.
(Buttons appear on the cloak.)

WEST WIND And a little braid at the hem?

KAREN Braid would be lovely.

SHEARS Braid braid braid braid braid braid.
(Braid appears on the cloak. The sound of the wind rises.)

WEST WIND *(shouting)* Do you want pockets?

KAREN *(shouting)* Oh, yes!

SHEARS Lockets lockets lockets lockets lockets.

> *(A shower of lockets appears.)*

WEST WIND What's this? Lockets? I said pockets, not lockets.

SHEARS Pockets pockets pockets pockets pockets.

WEST WIND That's better. Now you're dressed for traveling. Keep my Golden Shears for yourself, daughter. You never know when they'll come in handy.

KAREN Oh, I can't take your Shears. Won't you need them for sewing?

EAST WIND You'll need them more.

KAREN Well, thank you. That's very kind of you.

EAST WIND Take good care of her, sister.

WEST WIND Don't worry. I take good care of everyone.

KAREN Shall I climb on your cloak?

WEST WIND Cloak schmoak. What do I need a cloak for when I have— wi-i-i-i-ings? *(She unfurls her magnificent wings.)*

BIRDS Good-bye, good-bye!

KAREN Good-bye!

RAVEN Give my regards to the Trolls!

> *(The Stars go out, darkness falls.)*

Scene II

> *Sound of howling wind. Lights up on the North Wind's house. Karen and the West Wind arrive. The North Wind is doing push-ups.*

NORTH WIND *BLAST YOU BOTH, WHAT DO YOU WANT?*

WEST WIND You needn't be so foul. Here I am, your own sister, coming to see you.

NORTH WIND What do you want to borrow?

WEST WIND Nothing!

NORTH WIND You want me to make a molehill out of a mountain? Move a river? Bury a desert?

WEST WIND No—I—

NORTH WIND You want me to send you a glacier of ice cream?

WEST WIND I don't want anything for myself, brother. But this girl here—

NORTH WIND Where did *she* come from? *(He picks Karen up and whirls her around.)* Why, she's as light as a feather.

KAREN Please—put me down!

WEST WIND She's little, but she's strong. She's crossed seven oceans and seven deserts to find you.

NORTH WIND Hmmm. Is she one of the Bird people?

WEST WIND No. She's a human being—she's the lass who ought to have had the Prince that's gone east of the sun and west of the moon. And she wants to ask you something. *(To Karen)* Go ahead, ask him while he's in a good humor.

KAREN Can you tell me the way to the Trolls' castle?

NORTH WIND I know well enough where it is. Once in my life I blew an aspen leaf there, and I was so tired I couldn't blow a puff for ever so many days afterwards. You don't want to go that far, a little bit of a thing like you.

KAREN Yes, I do.

NORTH WIND You'll get seasick, homesick, heartsick.

KAREN No, I won't.

NORTH WIND You'll get tired and scared. Then you'll start to cry. Then you'll start to whimper. Then you'll start to yell, "Take me home, take me home!"

KAREN I won't.

NORTH WIND Even when hundreds of ships start sinking?

KAREN No.

NORTH WIND Even when my wings start drooping?

KAREN No.

NORTH WIND Even when the Trolls roar? Not even then?

KAREN N—no.

NORTH WIND I've never met anyone so stubborn.

KAREN Oh, please. I promise not to cause any trouble.

NORTH WIND Very well, I'll carry you. But you must sleep here tonight. We need the whole day before us if we're to get there at all.

North Wind

WEST WIND Hang on tight, Karen. My brother never waits for stragglers.

KAREN I will.

NORTH WIND And if you start whining, I'll dump you in the North Sea.

> (*Lights out on the North Wind, the West Wind, and Karen.*)

Scene III

> *Lights up on puppets of Karen and the North Wind flying over the water.*

EAST WIND, WEST WIND, SOUTH WIND (*sing*)
> Lullaby, my travelers,
> You have journeyed far.
> East of the farthest ocean,
> West of the nearest star.

SOUTH WIND Sisters, look! Our brother's wings are brushing the waves—

WEST WIND He must be totally exhausted.

EAST WIND The water is dashing over his heels—

WEST WIND His cloak is dripping with water—

NORTH WIND Are you afraid, Karen?

KAREN No!

NORTH WIND There's the castle. I've just enough strength to toss you ashore. Every part of me aches.

KAREN What are those ugly beasts?

NORTH WIND Those are the Trolls.

KAREN Is that Longnose I see on the balcony?

NORTH WIND It is. Listen.

Scene IV

> *Lights up on the Trolls' castle. It has a prominent balcony, and the castle rises from a strip of shore. Longnose appears on the balcony. The sea sparkles in the distance.*

VOICE OF THE TROLL QUEEN Longnose, clean your room!

LONGNOSE Clean it yourself, you old hag.

NORTH WIND Pleasant, aren't they?

KAREN Who are those people watching us from the tower?

NORTH WIND The Captives. Take care that the Trolls don't lock *you* in the tower. You'll never get out if they do.

KAREN Won't you come with me?

NORTH WIND No, I'm too old for such adventures. Too old and too tired. I'll have to sleep for three days before I can make the trip back. There must be a good cave among these rocks. (*He wanders off to find it.*)

(*Longnose stands on the balcony of the castle. Karen looks up at her from the shore.*)

LONGNOSE (*sings*)
When you're waiting for your wedding,
never ask for less
than a hundred Captives
to make your wedding dress.
I want rings of silver,
never bought or sold,
I want emerald ice cream
and applesauce of gold.

(*She gives an evil laugh.*)

KAREN (*To the audience*) I wonder if Trolls like apples? It's worth a try.

(*Karen strolls on the shore under the balcony, tossing the Golden Apple from one hand to the other.*)

LONGNOSE Hey, what's that you've got, beggar girl?

KAREN A Golden Apple. Isn't it beautiful? And it's the only Golden Apple in the world. (*She holds it up.*)

LONGNOSE Not bad. What do you want for it?

KAREN I won't sell it for gold or silver.

LONGNOSE Then what *will* you sell it for? Name your price.

KAREN Is this the house of the Prince who's to be married in three days?

LONGNOSE It is.

KAREN I've always wanted to see a Prince. Let me slip into his room tonight, and the Apple is yours.

LONGNOSE You want to look at the Prince? (*To the audience*) What a dumbbell. (*To Karen*) It's a deal. Go round to the back door.

TROLL QUEEN   Longnose! Longnose!

LONGNOSE   Here, Mother. Look at what I bought from the beggar girl.

MOTHER   My clever daughter. What'd you pay for it?

LONGNOSE   What she asked.

TROLL QUEEN   And what did she ask?

LONGNOSE   She wants to slip into the Prince's room tonight.

TROLL QUEEN   And you're going to let her?

LONGNOSE   Of course. Look at this Apple. *(imitating Karen)* Isn't it beautiful? It's the only Golden Apple in the world.

TROLL QUEEN   Are you crazy? The Prince will run away with her.

LONGNOSE   *(sings, does a little Troll two-step)*
>   He won't run away, he can't run away.
>   I'll give him a drink to make him sleep.
>   Let the girl howl, let the girl weep,
>   I'll give him a drink to make him snore.
>   Let the girl holler and pound on the door,
>   let the girl holler and shout all night.
>   He won't wake up till the morning light.

TROLL QUEEN   My clever daughter.

LONGNOSE   Tonight we'll add her to our collection of Captives.

(They laugh together.)

Scene V

Lights up on the Prince's room. The Prince is asleep. A ruby goblet stands on the table by his bed.

WEST WIND   The Prince's room is a drafty hall.

SOUTH WIND   If he'd press his ear to the farthest wall, he could hear the Captives murmur and cry.

(Murmurs and cries grow louder. The back wall becomes transparent. The Captives can be seen on the other side.)

EAST WIND   He'd hear them whisper, he'd hear them sigh.

(Cries turn to whispers.)

The Trolls' Castle

NORTH WIND   That's where the Trolls will take Karen unless he wakes—

> (Enter Karen. The Captives grow still.)

KAREN   Prince, I've found you! Oh, I've found you! Wake up. I've come such a long way. We'll run away together. Wake up!

CAPTIVE 1   What's that roaring and weeping?

CAPTIVE 2   It doesn't sound like the Troll Princess.

CAPTIVE 3   It doesn't even sound like a Troll.

KAREN   Wake up, wake up, please wake up—

> (Enter the Troll Queen and Longnose.)

LONGNOSE   Your time's up, your time's up! Out with you, out with you!

KAREN   Oh, please. Just a few minutes more—

TROLL QUEEN   Out with you!

> (The Troll Queen and Longnose hustle Karen out of the room. The Prince gives a snore.)

TROLL QUEEN   An earthquake wouldn't wake him.

LONGNOSE   Now can we throw the beggar girl in with the other Captives?

TROLL QUEEN   No, not yet. Let her try to escape first.

LONGNOSE   Oh, what fun that will be! Our Troll-ship sits in the harbor, but as long as we live, she'll never find it.

Scene VI

> Lights up on the outside of the castle. Karen walks under the balcony, as before, playing with the Golden Comb.

KAREN   I hate to give you up, my lovely Comb. I don't have many pretty things left. (She combs her hair, and roses fall out of it.)

TROLL QUEEN   Look at that! What a handy thing that would be for the wedding. You need a bouquet, and flowers are so hard to come by here.

LONGNOSE   The flowers I touch always turn into toads.

TROLL QUEEN   But the Prince loves flowers. You must have that Comb. Let's see what she'll take for it.

LONGNOSE   Hey, what do you want for your Golden Comb?

KAREN   It's not for sale for silver or gold.

LONGNOSE   Name your price.

KAREN   If I can spend another night in the Prince's room, I'll give you the Comb.

TROLL QUEEN   What a dummy!

LONGNOSE   She can spend a hundred nights in the Prince's room, for all I care. My magic sleeping potion could put an ocean to sleep. *(Calls to Karen)* It's a deal. Throw me the Comb.

(Karen throws it, and Longnose combs her hair.)

LONGNOSE   Look Ma, no toads!

TROLL QUEEN   But no flowers, either. Nothing but poison ivy. Keep combing.

LONGNOSE   Now it's onions and garlic.

TROLL QUEEN   Not bad. Keep combing.

LONGNOSE   Now it's dandelions.

TROLL QUEEN   All it takes is a little practice. By your wedding day, everything will be coming up roses.

Scene VII

Lights up on the Prince's room.

KAREN   Wake up, wake up, please wake up.

ECHO   Wake up wake up wake up wake up wake up . . .

CAPTIVE 1   Two nights running! Who can she be?

CAPTIVE 2   Why does the Prince sleep so soundly?

CAPTIVE 3   Her cries could raise the dead.

KAREN   Wake up, wake up, wake up . . .

(Enter Longnose.)

LONGNOSE   Your time's up, your time's up!

KAREN   Please—can't I stay—

LONGNOSE   Out the door with you, beggar girl!

(Longnose hustles Karen out. The Prince yawns and stretches. Longnose turns to the Prince.)

Wake up, my sweetheart! Wake up, my honey!

PRINCE   What time is it? What day is it?

LONGNOSE   It's the day before our wedding.

(The Prince groans. He sits on the edge of the bed with his head in his hands.)

You should see the cake. It's taller than I am.

PRINCE This is awful.

LONGNOSE Oh, no, it's delicious. This cake is an old Troll recipe, a real specialty. Gold nuggets baked in sea slime. You won't find it anywhere else out of the world.

PRINCE Ugh.

LONGNOSE What did you say?

PRINCE Nothing. Nothing important.

LONGNOSE And the frosting on the cake is this thick. *(She measures with her hands—a foot high.)* My wedding cake is frosted with diamonds and broccoli.

PRINCE Real diamonds? You eat them?

LONGNOSE Nobody eats diamonds, stupid. They're just for show. Speaking of show, you should see my dress. *(The Prince looks at her dress.)* Not this dress, stupid. My wedding dress.

PRINCE And what's your wedding dress made of? Toads?

LONGNOSE Gossamer and silk. It's a dream.

PRINCE You know, I had the strangest dream last night. And when I woke up, I thought for a moment it was true.

LONGNOSE Dreams don't come true.

PRINCE Well, I'm not dreaming now, that's for sure.

LONGNOSE Get dressed and come down as soon as you can. My father killed a dragon last night, and we're having it for breakfast.

PRINCE *(to himself)* And for lunch, and for dinner. Dragon sandwiches, dragon soup, dragon casserole . . .

LONGNOSE If you don't hurry, you won't get so much as a bone to chew on. You know my family.

(Exit Longnose.)

PRINCE *(to himself)* It was only a dream. And dreams don't come true.

CAPTIVE 1 Sometimes they do.

PRINCE Who said that? Where are you?

CAPTIVES We're here, on the other side of the wall.

The Troll Queen and Longnose

CAPTIVE 1 We're the Trolls' Captives.

PRINCE Captives?

CAPTIVE 1 Haven't you seen us at the window?

CAPTIVE 2 Haven't you heard us weeping?

CAPTIVE 3 Prince, why do you sleep so deeply?

PRINCE I don't sleep deeply.

CAPTIVE 3 Oh, but you do. Every night a girl comes to your room and tries to wake you—

CAPTIVE 1 She roars and weeps—

CAPTIVE 2 No one can sleep—

CAPTIVE 3 For her wailing and calling.

CAPTIVE 1 *(imitating Karen)* Wake up, please wake up—

PRINCE Is this true?

CAPTIVE 1 Stay awake tonight, and you'll see if it's true or not.

PRINCE *(Picking up the ruby goblet and sniffing it)* I thought that stuff Longnose gave me to drink tasted odd. And it made me so terribly tired.

Scene VIII

Lights up on the castle. The Troll Queen bustles out to the balcony.

TROLL QUEEN Longnose! Longnose! Ah, there's so much to do. The King can't find his shoes. Longnose spilled grease on her gown. Nobody has the right clothes.

LONGNOSE *(Joining her mother on the balcony)* My dress is a mess. I tore it on the stairs.

TROLL QUEEN I don't know why you can't learn to sew. Do I have to do everything for you?

(Karen walks under the balcony, clipping with the Golden Shears, from which small dresses fall.)

KAREN Good-bye, little Shears. You're my last hope. *(sings)*
Clip, clip, clip!
Throw away your sorrow.
The wedding day's tomorrow.
Make a dainty veil

Never found for sale.
Make a wedding gown,
Loveliest in town.
Clip, clip, clip!

TROLL QUEEN What now?

LONGNOSE Look! Look what the beggar girl's got for sale.

TROLL QUEEN Magic Shears. They're just what we need.

LONGNOSE What's the price of those Shears, beggar girl? The same as before, I suppose. A night with the Prince.

KAREN One more night.

LONGNOSE And it'll be your last, my girl, because tomorrow we're to be married.

KAREN One more night with the Prince and the Shears are yours.

LONGNOSE A bargain!

Scene IX

Lights up on the Prince's room. The Prince sits by the window with his head in his hands. Enter Longnose with goblet.

LONGNOSE A lovely drink for you. Let's toast to our future happiness.

PRINCE A toast. *(He raises his glass.)* Oh, look out the window. Who's that girl outside?

LONGNOSE Where? *(The Prince throws out his drink.)* I see no girl.

PRINCE My eyes are playing tricks on me.

LONGNOSE Too much excitement. Because of the wedding tomorrow.

PRINCE Ah, yes, the wedding.

LONGNOSE Wait till you see my dress. Wait till you see the flowers in my hair.

PRINCE Why am I so sleepy? I can hardly keep my eyes open.

LONGNOSE Good night, sweetheart. Tomorrow you'll be mine forever.

(The Prince pretends to sleep. Longnose leaves. Karen approaches.)

KAREN Wake up, wake up—

PRINCE Karen, my dear Karen, is it really you?

KAREN It's really me.

PRINCE You've come just in time. Tomorrow's the wedding. You're the only woman who can set me free.

KAREN Of course I'll set you free. But how?

PRINCE Listen, I have an idea. Just before the wedding when the Trolls have all gathered, I'll say I want to see what my wife is fit for, and I'll tell Longnose to wash these three spots of wax out of my shirt.

KAREN Oh, those three spots. If only I had listened to you instead of my mother.

PRINCE I'll tell the Trolls that I won't marry anyone but the woman who can wash that shirt clean.

KAREN And what if Longnose washes it clean?

PRINCE She won't.

KAREN How can you be so sure?

PRINCE Because only the person who made those spots can wash them out. You're the only person, Karen, who can do that.

Scene X

Lights down on the Prince's room, lights up on the front of the stage. The Trolls are dancing. Gradually the lights rise on the Prince's room, and the Trolls enter.

TROLL KING Hurry up with the wedding so we can get to the cake.

TROLL QUEEN Welcome to the family, Prince. You're getting a wonderful wife.

PRINCE Wait a minute. I have a favor to ask of my bride.

LONGNOSE Ask away.

PRINCE I've got this fine shirt which I'd like to wear for my wedding, but somehow or other it has got three spots of wax on it.

TROLL QUEEN Wax?

PRINCE Three spots. They won't wash out. I've tried everything.

TROLL QUEEN My daughter can make you another one right away. She can sew anything in two seconds.

PRINCE I'll have no other bride than the woman who can wash out these three spots. If she can't do that, she's not worth having.

TROLL QUEEN Well, three spots of wax—that's no great thing.

The Troll King

LONGNOSE   No great thing.

TROLL QUEEN   Fetch a washtub.

CAPTIVES   *(chanting from the other side of the wall)*
> Longnose, Longnose!
> The more you wash, the worse it grows.
> The spots are big as apples,
> the spots are big as pears;
> it rips, ravels, and tears.
> Longnose, Longnose,
> the more you wash, the worse it grows.

TROLL QUEEN   Let me try. *(She scrubs and scrubs.)* Look—it's almost clean.

PRINCE   Why, the shirt is as black as if you'd dragged it through the chimney.

TROLL QUEEN   That's not dirt. That's a shadow.

TROLL GUESTS   Let me try, let me try!

> *(With much jostling and grabbing, the Trolls pass the shirt around. Each takes a turn at scrubbing.)*

CAPTIVES   It still shows, it still shows,
> the more you wash, the worse it grows.
> Black as dirt, black as soot,
> black as the bottom of your foot,
> Longnose, Longnose!

PRINCE   Ah, you're none of you worth a straw. You can't even wash a shirt. There's a beggar girl outside. I'll bet she can wash better than the whole lot of you. Come in, girl!

> *(Karen comes in.)*

KAREN   What do you want, sir?

PRINCE   Can you wash this shirt clean?

KAREN   I don't know. I'll try. *(She washes it clean.)*

PRINCE   You're the bride for me.

LONGNOSE   No, no, no, no, no!

TROLL QUEEN   We've been tricked!

> *(A gong sounds, and the Trolls freeze. Lights out. A burst of dissonant music, during which Trolls exit.)*